Dear mouse  welcome to the world of

Geronimo Stilton

The Editorial Staff of
The Rodent's Gazette

1. Linda Thinslice
2. Sweetie Cheesetriangle
3. Ratella Redfur
4. Soya Mousehao
5. Cheesita de la Pampa
6. Mouseanna Mousetti
7. Yale Youngmouse
8. Toni Tinypaw
9. Tina Spicytail
10. Maximilian Mousemower
11. Valerie Vole
12. Trap Stilton
13. Branwen Musclemouse
14. Zeppola Zap
15. Merenguita Gingermouse
16. Ratsy O'Shea
17. Rodentrick Roundrat
18. Tillie von Muffler
19. Thea Stilton
20. Erronea Misprint
21. Pinky Pick
22. Ya-ya O'Cheddar
23. Mousella Mac Mouser
24. Kreamy O'Cheddar
25. Blasco Tabasco
26. Toffie Sugarsweet
27. Tylerat Truemouse
28. Larry Keys
29. Michael Mouse
30. Geronimo Stilton
31. Benjamin Stilton
32. Briette Finerat
33. Raclette Finerat

Geronimo Stilton
A learned and brainy
mouse, editor of
The Rodent's Gazette

Thea Stilton
Geronimo's sister and
special correspondent at
The Rodent's Gazette

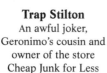

Trap Stilton
An awful joker,
Geronimo's cousin and
owner of the store
Cheap Junk for Less

Benjamin Stilton
A sweet and loving
nine-year-old mouse.
Geronimo's favorite
nephew

Geronimo Stilton

LOST TREASURE OF THE EMERALD EYE

Scholastic Inc.

New York   Toronto   London   Auckland   Sydney

Mexico City   New Delhi   Hong Kong   Buenos Aires

ISBN 0-439-55963-4

Text by Geronimo Stilton
Original cover by Matt Wolf, revised by Larry Keys
Illustrations by Matt Wolf, Mark Nithael, and Kat Stevens
Graphics by Merenguita Gingermouse, Angela Simone, and Benedetta Galante
Special thanks to Kathryn Cristaldi
Cover design by Ursula Albano
Interior layout by Robin Camera

Printed in the U.S.A.
First printing, February 2004

12 11 10 9   7 8 9/0

LATE AGAIN!

"Putrid cheese puffs!" It was nine o'clock and I, Geronimo Stilton, was late for work — again! I rolled out of bed in a minute and was dressed in two. Pretty fast, considering I am really not a morning mouse.

"CHEESE SLICES! I hate Monday mornings," I grumbled while brushing my teeth with cheddar-flavored toothpaste. Then I hurried downstairs, stumbled over my tail, and tumbled all the way down to the door.

Thump! Thump! Thump! So much for being quiet as a mouse.

The streets of New Mouse City, the capital of Mouse Island, were as noisy as ever. I guess everyone was late just like me. Cheese delivery trucks were everywhere, horns blasting. Mice, rats, and rodents of every size and shape *raced by* in cars, taxis, and Mouse Jordan sneakers.

"Taxi!" I shouted, jumping into a cab. "Seventeen Swiss Cheese Center."

Minutes later, we pulled up to my editorial office. Oh, yes, I forgot to tell you that I run a newspaper. It's called *The Rodent's Gazette*.

I took the stairs two at a time and burst inside. What a workout! I was *pooped*. Maybe I shouldn't have canceled my membership at Rats La Lanne after all.

But before I could think about it, Mousella,
my secretary, tackled me.

"*Mr. Stilton,* **FINALLY!**" she cried, her glasses dangling off one ear. "There is a crowd of rodents waiting to see you: the designers, the printers, the mouse who works the water cooler . . . and the editor in chief wants to speak with you **immediately**."

I headed to my desk. Mousella followed.

"The copy machine is jammed," she continued. "Another mailroom mouse quit. And, Boss, *don't forget you promised me a raise!*"

My head felt like it was about to explode. Even my whiskers hurt. I wouldn't wish this day on the meanest  ever!

I hate Mondays. . . .

THEA'S SECRET

At lunchtime, my sister, Thea, who is a special correspondent for *The Rodent's Gazette,* came by on her motorcycle.

"I am taking you out to lunch," she said. "We've got reservations at The Mouse House." She grabbed my paw and whispered, "I have to tell you a very important secret."

TWENTY MINUTES later, I peeled myself off Thea's motorcycle. My teeth were still chattering.

"Are you trying to give me a heart attack?" I shrieked, tugging my whiskers back into shape. "why, why, why do you have to go so fast? It's dangerous! One day, we're going to end up sipping cheese through straws at Mouse General!!"

"*Tsk, tsk* . . . still the same old 'fraidy mouse." My sister laughed, slipping into the restaurant.

Tsk
Tsk

Of course, before we could sit down, Thea had to greet fifty friends.

"Hi, Ratsy! How you doing, Swissita!"

I rolled my eyes. Thea had more friends than a cheese delivery man the day before Thanksgiving!

Finally, we were seated.

"So what is it?" I asked impatiently.

But my sister was busy looking at the menu. "Why don't we order first," she said. "Cheddar ravioli for two!" she told the waiter. "With *extra-spicy* tomato sauce."

"Spicy?" I groaned. "You know I get **HEARTBURN**." Did I mention my sister can be incredibly annoying at times?

Thea waved her paw. "Oh, please. You could use a little spice in your life. Besides, you'll have to get used to eating all sorts of food on *our trip*," she whispered, winking at me.

"Trip? What trip?" I asked.

"**Sssssssh!** *Sssssssh!* Do you want everybody to know?" she said, pinching my tail.

"Well, what are you talking about?" I hissed.

Thea glanced around. "Hold your whiskers. I think the waiter may be spying on us. He looks a little suspicious," she said.

"Who on earth would want to spy on us?" I cried. My head started to pound.

"If you only knew . . ." my sister replied, looking very mysterious.

I clenched my fists. I couldn't take it anymore. I climbed onto my chair and screamed, "**WHAT ARE YOU TALKING ABOUT?!**"

Everyone stared.

"**Slimy Swiss balls!** Someone got up on the wrong side of the hole today," said Thea. But she began talking anyway. "I found a map of an island showing the spot

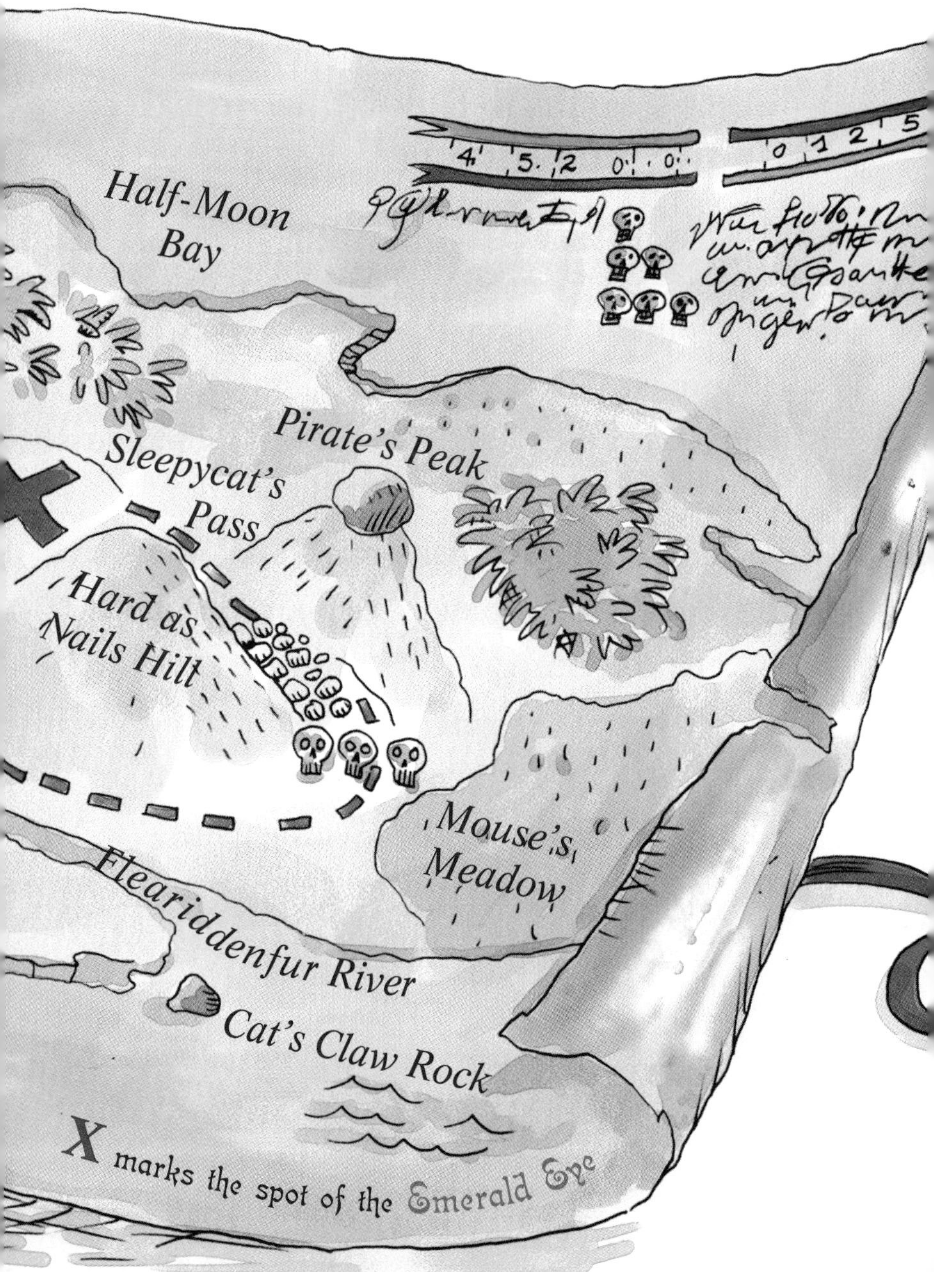

Half-Moon Bay

Pirate's Peak

Sleepycat's Pass

Hard as Nails Hill

Mouse's Meadow

Fleariddenfur River

Cat's Claw Rock

X marks the spot of the Emerald Eye

where treasure is buried," she squeaked. *"The Emerald Eye!"*

From under the table she pulled out a YELLOWED piece of paper.

"I found this map at the flea market," she continued. "Oh, **GERRYKINS**, you must come with me. This is a once-in-a-lifetime chance!" she finished excitedly.

"First of all, don't call me **GERRYKINS**. My name is Geronimo!" I cried. "Second, I will be too busy at work. We are about to publish the next volume of *RODENT RULES FOR DUMMIES*. And besides, who ever heard of an *Emerald Eye*? It's ridiculous!"

Thea grabbed my paw and stared straight into my eyes. "But you're my **big** brother — you can't let me go on my own, GERRY BERRY!" she squeaked in her sweetest voice. My sister could

convince a cat to cook dinner for her.

"The name is **GE-RO-NI-MO**!" I shouted.

That night, I drank about ten cups of snoozytime tea, listened to my squeaky-sounds sleep tape, and counted grilled cheese sandwiches. Still, I didn't sleep one wink!

CHEAP JUNK
FOR LESS

The next day, we went to the harbor.

"So, **GERRYKINS**, promise you'll come with me. You are not going to let me sail off all on my own!" insisted Thea.

"Don't call me **GERRYKINS**," I cried. "The name is Ge-ro-ni-mo!"

Here's one thing you should know about my sister. When she gets an **idea** in her head, it sticks

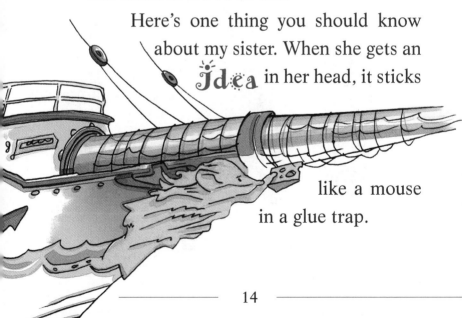

like a mouse in a glue trap.

Before I knew it, I had promised to go with her on her ridiculous treasure-hunting trip. And as every respectable mouse knows, a rodent's promise is nothing to joke about.

"**CHEWY CHEESE BITS!**" shouted Thea, breaking into a dance.

Then Thea showed me a boat belonging to an old retired sea captain. It was the color of cheddar, extra-sharp, my favorite. The ship's name seemed to be a good sign, too: *Lucky Lady*.

My sister stared at the ship, then she winked at me. "You know, two sailors are really not enough for this boat," she said. "Do you know who else could come with us? Trap! He says he's an expert **SAILOR!**"

SAILOR! SAILOR! SAILOR! SAILOR!

My memories of my cousin Trap

Stilton, also known as Pushy Paws, were not very good. When he was young, he was a real nightmare.

"Trap?!" I sputtered. "But, Thea, don't you remember when he tied my tail up in a knot? I had to wear the same pants for a week! And what about the time he dyed my whiskers with that **purple grape juice?**"

But as I said, when my sister gets an idea in her head, there's no stopping her. Minutes later, we stood in front of Trap's thrift shop, Cheap Junk for Less. The store window was dusty and full of odd stuff: an old, YELLOWED photograph, a fake crystal that was supposed to ward off cats, a box of silver whisker-curlers, a super-powered fur dryer.

We went in. As the door opened, it

triggered a bunch of small brass bells hanging from the ceiling. Inside, a **PLUMPiSH** mouse with short paws and a pencil tucked behind his ear sat with his feet up on

a **comfy** reclining chair. He wore baggy blue pants and a pair of bright-red suspenders. It was Trap. He **leaped** up and scurried toward us with surprising speed.

"Well, I'll be a mouse's uncle!" he shouted, crushing my paw in his. "Long time no see! You two are always together, huh? Like cream and cheese. So what's up? Want to buy something? Let me tell you

right up front: no discounts. Not even to relatives! cash only!" he shouted in our ears.

"Is there somewhere quiet we can talk?" asked Thea.

Trap led us into a library filled with books on every subject. Cats. Cheese. Cats who eat cheese and the mice who love them. The air SMELLED musty, as if the windows hadn't been opened since Christopher Columouse discovered Mouse Island.

All of a sudden, we heard a horrifying sound. Meeeooowwww!!!

Thea and I leaped up in the air.

"**CAT!!!**" we shrieked together.

Trap rolled around on the floor in a fit of laughter.

"Ha! Ha! Ha!" he sputtered. "That's no cat. It's just a tape recording. It comes on automatically as soon as someone enters the library. Pretty cute, don't you think?"

"Adorable," squeaked Thea, ROLLING HER EYES.

"Well, it does keep rat burglars away, and slimy sewer rats, too!" smirked Trap. "Hmm . . . I wonder if I could take out a patent on it," he added. I could just hear the wheels turning in his tiny mouse-sized brain.

"I could make a bundle," he mumbled, his eyes shining. Then he turned back to us.

WWWWwwwwwww!!!!

"So anyway, what are you two looking for? I don't have much time to shoot the cheese. I'm a very busy mouse, you know," he added with pride, puffing up his fur.

Trap listened to Thea's plans with half-closed eyes. But I could tell he was interested because his tail started to twitch when she mentioned the Emerald Eye.

"OK, I'll join you," he agreed. "But anyone who dares to lay a paw on my part of the treasure is a dead rat!"

We toasted to a successful trip, and twisting our tails together we squeaked: "To our trip!

Friends together! Mice forever!,"

TAKE ME WITH YOU!

On my way home, I stopped by to say hello to my favorite nephew, Benjamin. He's a cute **little guy** with tiny flappy ears.

"Uncle, read me a story!" he cried when he saw me. So I **SAT DOWN** in the big, comfy chair in the den.

Ben loves stories. When he was younger, he always zonked out before I had a chance to finish my tale. That's why I dedicated my book *Stilton's Cheesy Tales for Tiny Mice* to him.

"To Ben," I wrote. *"May you stay awake long enough to finish this book!"*

Today I can hardly believe my little nephew is already nine years old! I remember when he was just a squeaky little thing, drinking cheese sauce from a baby bottle!

"You're going on a trip?" Ben asked when he heard about my plans. "Oh, please, please, please take me with you, Uncle! I can be your assistant. I can carry your notebooks. And I can sharpen your pencils with my cat-tooth pencil sharpener," he pleaded.

"Sorry, Ben," I said, ruffling his fur. "Maybe next time, when you're a little older."

Then I laid my right paw on my HĖART
and tugged at my whi**s**kers with my left
paw. This is a salute that we mice use
on *special occasions*. It means that the
HĖARTS of two mice who love
each other will always stay connected.

The hearts of two mice who love each other will always stay connected.

ANYTHING MISSING?

Fifteen pounds of extra-sharp cheddar

eighty boxes of mac and cheese

ten tubs of Swiss

nine bags of nacho cheese chips, unsalted...

The next morning, I stood on the deck of the *Lucky Lady*, reading **out** a list of our supplies. What a mess!

"Trap, fill up the water tank," I instructed my cousin, but instead of filling the water tank, he poured water into the fuel tank! "What are you doing?!" I squeaked. "I think you had better lay off the extra-sharp — it seems to be affecting your brain!"

I turned to my sister.

"Thea, *run* and get me the compass I ordered down at Boats, Masts, and Beyond. Ask to see the owner, **Squeaky La Rue**, also known as **The Squeak**. He's a friend of mine, so he should give you a discount. You can't miss him. He's a tall, thin, gray mouse with a tail so furry you could use it to dust every room in your mousehole."

Just then I noticed Trap *talking* to the young ship rat on the boat next to ours.

"That's right, my young rat friend,"

he whispered. "Don't tell anyone . . . we're looking for something but I can't tell you what. . . . It begins with a T and ends with an E. . . . That's right, it's on an island."

Quick as a cat at a mouse convention, I leaped up and yanked Trap away by the tail. "Are you going to blurt out the whole story about the treasure?" I *hissed*.

Trap gave me an innocent smile. "Did **I** mention a treasure? There are lots of words that begin with **T** and end with **E**, you know," he smirked. "Telephone, for example. Or how about ticktacktoe?"

I banged my head against the side of the ship.

By six o'clock that night, we had finished loading. I rushed to **Rats Authority**, the best store in town for sporting goods.

"Can you help me, please?" I said to

Scratch, the mouse who owns the place. "I want to get everything I would need for a long sea voyage. And I'm in a big rush, so if you could hurry . . ."

"Well, tickle me with a cat-fur feather! If it isn't *Geronimo Stilton*, the newspaper mouse!" Scratch cried. "What an honor!"

He then began to drag out **ev-er-y-thing** in the entire store. My head was spinning. There were ten pairs of waterproof under-wear, a floppy cheddar-colored straw hat that squeaked if you stayed out in the sun too long, and a life raft shaped like a slice of cheese on a five-foot-long cracker.

"I also need a suitcase," I said to Scratch. "Or better yet, a big trunk!"

"I've got just the thing for a sharp mouse like you, Mr. Stilton!" he remarked, his eyes gleaming. "Follow me."

He led me to the back of the store, where he unlocked the door to a small room. Then, like the famous magician Harry Ratini, he lifted a silk cloth with a flourish.

There stood a trunk as TALL as a circus mouse on stilts. It was covered in bright YELLOW leather that glowed in the dark. It was as **wide** as the giant from *Rat and the Beanstalk* and as **long** as the line for cheese danish at the bakery on Sunday morning.

"Isn't it a beauty?" asked Scratch.

I nodded and **carefully** lifted the lid. Holey cheese! You could fit a sumo mouse inside!

I spotted several coat hangers made of cheese cloth and a whole shelf just for hats. There was a shiny cat-tooth comb and a wire brush for tough whiskers. The trunk also had a space for office supplies: paper, pens, paperweights, a tiny, tiny secret compartment, you name it.

"I'll take it!" I **SQUEAKED**.

"I knew you would like it, *Mr. Stilton!* This is the real deal." He beamed, running his paws over the trunk. "*It's just the thing for an adventurous seagoing mouse such as yourself. Wish you could take me along.*"

Hmm. Geronimo Stilton: Fearless Sailor of the High Seas, I thought. Had a nice ring to it. I just might enjoy this trip after all!

…Ahh, that salty smell of seaweed!

FIRST DAWN AT SEA

Ahh, the *cool breeze* blowing in off the sea . . . Ahh, that salty smell of seaweed . . .

I was starting to get into this sailing thing. It was so relaxing. Sort of like sitting in Great Grandma Tanglefur's rocking chair. **Holding** the tiller of the *Lucky Lady* in my paws, I stared out over the ocean waves. It was dawn, and the sun was just coming up, pale as a slice of Swiss cheese.

We had just left the harbor, but I felt as if I'd been sailing all my life! I was wearing a bright yellow windbreaker jacket with matching yellow pants and my new yellow hat.

Can you guess what my favorite color is? Yep, there's nothing like a little yellow to **cheer up** a mouse. It is the most popular color on our island. We have yellow cars, yellow schools, and yellow airplanes. In fact, one year, even Santa Mouse wore a **YELLOW SUIT** instead of a red one! My nephew Ben wasn't too crazy about that, though.

I smiled. I missed Ben so much. Funny how such a small mouse could give you **such a big heartache!**

My daydreams were interrupted by Trap. He appeared on deck **munching** on a bag of nacho cheese chips.

"Hey there, Cousin," he squeaked with his mouth full. "Want some?"

"Be careful!" I warned. "Don't get any grease on the deck!"

"You're such a **WORRYWART**," he muttered, laying his greasy paw right on the deck.

I closed my eyes and counted to ten.

"Just bring me my chart." I sighed. "I need to see if we are on course for Treasure Island."

"Hey, no problemo, my little cousin!" squeaked Trap, waving a life buoy at me. He did a little dance.

"**LOOK out!**" I shrieked.

"You almost stepped on my glasses!" I broke out in a COLD SWEAT. Without my glasses, I couldn't tell the difference between a slice of mozzarella and a hunk of **cheddar!** **Why, oh, why** had we brought him along?

FRESH CLAMS, ANYONE?

It was evening, and the red **sun** sat on the ocean like a **cherry** on top of a piece of cheesecake. Up in the sky, white fluffy clouds of whipped cream floated around.

"What a *delicious* view!" I sighed.

But just as I was beginning to enjoy it, I heard a mouse screaming.

"Yeowee! That rotten stove is trying to kill me!" It was my cousin's voice.

Thea and I rushed to help him.

"What happened?

What is it?" we squeaked together.

Trap was leaping around on one paw. "This rotten stove keeps jumping **UP** and **DOWN** like a teenage mouse at a *Wild Whiskers* concert!" shrieked my cousin, massaging his toe. "I burned my paw with the clam sauce!" He slumped onto the padded sofa to check out his toe.

"Maybe you two can set the **TABLE**, at least," Trap continued. "While you've been up on deck enjoying the **FRESH** air, I've been busting my tail down here." He **closed** his eyes and yawned. "Must I do everything?"

I gave the clam sauce a good sniff as Thea mixed it into the pasta.

"Now I know why in medieval times they poured *boiling* oil on their enemies from the **CASTLE WALLS**," whined my cousin.

He cradled his burned paw protectively.

"Why, Trap, I didn't know you were so cultured!" I remarked, filling my plate.

My cousin smirked. "What culture? I got that from a cartoon on **TV**," he scoffed. "You can find everything on **TV**, you know."

"Yes, of course you can . . ." I answered absentmindedly. I was sniffing at the sauce again. "Are you sure these clams are fresh?"

"What do you mean, fresh? Of course they're **FRESH**!" Trap insisted. "*Cross my heart.*"

"It's just that they smell sort of like a SKUNK at a CHEAP PERFUME counter," I offered.

My cousin jumped off of the sofa. "Are you calling me a liar?" he shouted. "I told

you they were **FRESH AS FRESH** can be! If you don't believe me, fine. I guess you just enjoy hurting my feelings!"

Thea grabbed a slice of bread and headed for the stairs. "It's my turn to stand watch!" she chirped, RACING AWAY. I hesitated for a moment, then began to eat very slowly.

"I don't think I'll have any clams after all. I lost my appetite," said Trap, nibbling some bread and cheese.

At two o'clock that morning, I woke up with a *horrible stomachache.*

I dashed to the bathroom, my glasses dangling off my snout. Seconds later,

I tripped over the bath mat, **banged** my snout on the medicine cabinet, and plopped onto the toilet.

Suddenly, I had a horrible thought. *Could it be* the clams that had made me sick?

Just then the bathroom door opened wide. Looking half asleep, Trap peered into the bathroom. Then he covered his nose with both paws.

"What are you up to? Building some kind of **STINK BOMB**?" he coughed.

Thea, woken up by all the n**oise**, joined us. She sized up the situation in an instant.

"Spit out the truth, Trap," demanded my sister. "Where did you really buy those clams?"

My cousin was silent. He stared down at the carpet.

"Uh, well, I bought them in the fish department . . . at the **FROZEN-FOOD** counter!" he confessed with a guilty look.

"**FROZEN**?!" I squeaked. "But you told me they were **fresh** clams!"

Trap stood up straight. "Well, yes, of course they were **fresh** . . . at one time. The **FROZEN** clams were, um, a special offer. The mouse who sold them to me last month told me to eat them that same day or they would spoil . . . but, of course, I didn't take him seriously. You know these sales mice, they always tend to exaggerate," squeaked Trap.

"**Grrrrrr**. Sales mice, my paw!" I cried. "Do you realize you could have killed me with that poison?! You should get a job as a chef at a cafeteria for cats!"

I tried to grab him, but I ended up stumbling over a roll of toilet paper instead. Why, oh, **why** had we brought him along?

A MYSTERY
ON BOARD

At dawn, on the sixteenth day of sailing, we were almost *halfway to* Treasure Island. After my watch, I went down to the galley, where we had stored all of our food. That's when I discovered the bread crumbs on the floor.

Strange, very strange, I thought. The trail of crumbs led to a barrel full of **APPLES**. I lifted the barrel's lid.

Inside, I found five chewed-up apple cores!

Did we have a stowaway

on board? I decided not to say anything to the others. Not yet, anyway. If I was wrong, they would MAKE FUN OF ME FOR THE REST OF THE TRIP!

The next night, when everyone was asleep, I sprinkled some baby powder in front of the kitchen door. Then I tied a piece of thread to the doorknob.

Early the next morning I went down to check. Just as I'd thought! The thread had been broken! Yep, it sure looked like someone had been sticking their paws in the old Cheese Bit jar!

Then I noticed the paw prints in the

powder. How odd! They were very, very small. Could they belong to a dwarf mouse?

I decided I had to do something before the little thief ate us right out of houseboat and home! That night, I slept with my lucky baseball bat by my side. It was a present from **Slugrat Jones**, also known as Sluggy, an old rat friend of mine who plays professional baseball. If that stowaway came after me, I'd be ready for him!

It was one o'clock in the morning when I finally heard creaking sounds coming from

the kitchen. I put on my glasses. Then I grabbed a flashlight with my right paw and the bat with my left. When I got downstairs, the sneaky thief was opening the fridge. I tiptoed toward him and switched on the light.

"Aha!" I cried, ready to strike. Then my mouth dropped open. It was my nephew Benjamin, happily munching on a Cheesy Chew!

"Hello, Uncle!" he squeaked, flinging his

paws around my neck. He kissed me on the tip of my snout. "Aren't you glad to see me?"

"BUT WHY . . . BUT HOW . . . BUT WHEN . . .

I MEAN, WHAT ARE YOU DOING HERE?" I stammered.

"I promise to make myself useful!" he cried. "I'll sweep the deck, fold your clothes, stack your hats. Did you know I am a champion stacker? I got an A+ in stacking at Little Tails Academy when I was in kindergarten. And I'll be your secretary, too, so when you go back you can write a wonderful book!"

There was only one thing to do. I gave him a giant mouse hug.

"I love you very much, Benjamin," I said. "And I am very glad you are here!"

WHY... HOW... WHAT... WHEN...

Mouse Overboooard!

It was eleven o'clock at night, and I was standing watch at the helm.

"Everything all right, Geronimeister?" asked Thea.

"It would be even better if you didn't call me Geronimeister!" I squeaked.

It was getting colder. WAS THE WEATHER GOING TO CHANGE? I lifted my snout to look at the clouds, but just then the boat tipped and the boom hit me on the back. Before you could SAY "Grilled cheese on rye, hold the tomato!" I was knocked overboard. I didn't even have a chance to squeak! The boat sailed away from me as I floundered in the waves.

Fortunately, Thea had seen me go over. "Mouse overboooard!!" she shrieked. Immediately, all the lights came on, and the *Lucky Lady* turned toward me. Trap switched on a searchlight.

"**HELP!** Over here!" I cried, waving my paws. The waves were throwing me up and down like a Ratty Ann doll in a clothes dryer. Cold water seeped into my fur. My teeth began chattering so hard I thought they would bounce right out of my mouth.

"There he is!" I heard someone shout. Suddenly, I was flooded with light.

They had spotted me!

Benjamin threw me a line, but I couldn't catch it. Then I felt a strong paw grab me by the ears. It was Trap!

"Come on, Cousin! Grab hold of my tail!" he screamed.

He dragged me back to the *Lucky Lady*. Ben and Thea lowered a rope ladder.

Splat! I spat out a spray of water and opened my eyes. Trap was **jumping up** and down on my stomach.

"HE'S ALIVE ... HE'S **ALIVE!**" cried my cousin.

My ears were **BLUE** from the cold. Thea was holding my paw. Tears shone in her eyes.

"Uncle Trap, you really are a hero!" Ben exclaimed.

"Really, Trap, we don't know how to thank you!" Thea added gratefully.

Trap was blushing. "Oh, it's nothing, **ratlings**. Just another day for me. Don't mention it." He shrugged. He strode away, **WHISTLING** the theme song from his favorite TV show, *X-Mouse*.

What a character! Trap pretends to be tough, but he is really a total softie. In fact, I'd say he's just as soft as my aunt Ratilda's homemade cream cheese!

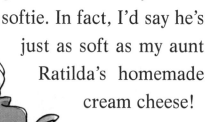

A True Sailor
Always Knows
What to Do

On the morning of the thirty-second day of sailing, I woke up with a start.

"Wake up, Gerrykins!" Thea shouted in my ear. "There's a storm out there!"

Still **Half asleep**, I slipped on my coat and followed Thea up to the deck. The sky in the east was dark with big black clouds!

"*Go* and lower the sails, Thea. No, wait a minute, leave the smallest one up. That way the boat will hold the seas better," I said. Maybe sailing wasn't such an easy thing after all.

"I'd better get Trap," I told my sister. "He's a true sailor. He'll know what to do."

I left Thea at the helm and went below to search for my cousin. The boat was being tossed about by the **churning** waves, which kept growing bigger and bigger.

I opened the door to Trap's cabin. My cousin was huddled up in his bunk under the covers.

"Trap, the _Lucky Lady_ is taking on water! We don't know what to do!" I shouted, shaking him.

"I . . . I . . . don't know, either!" he mumbled, rolling his eyes.

"B-B-B-ut," I sputtered, tossing my hat on his bed. "I thought you knew everything about the sea! Didn't you say you were once the captain of a ship?!"

In answer to my question, my cousin sat

up with a jolt and threw up right into my hat!

"*HOLEY CHEESE!*" I screamed, leaping away from the bed. I fell against Trap's closet. A book fell out. I stared at the title:

Learn How to Sail in Eight Hundred Easy Lessons.

A horrible feeling gripped me like a mousetrap in a fully stocked kitchen. I grabbed the book. A bookmark was stuck at page eleven. *Lesson number three: Sails come in many different colors. Try to pick one that will make you smile.*

"SMILE!" I choked. "You'll be lucky if

you can still eat soft cheeses when I'm through with you!" I screamed at Trap. He had crawled back under the covers. "I'll deal with you later!" I called as I rushed back outside.

Waves as high as Mouse Everest were pounding onto the deck. Each time the bow of the ship hit a wave, the boat sank lower. Then it would pop up again, this time tilted in the other direction. Trap wasn't the only one feeling seasick. I lurched over to my sister and gave her the bad news about our seriously truth-challenged cousin. For a minute, she looked as if she'd seen a cat. But she quickly got a grip. **"WHO NEEDS HIM ANYWAY?"** she squeaked, flipping her tail over her shoulder.

What a mouse, that sister of mine! A **FIRST-RATE** rodent, for sure.

The wind was getting stronger and stronger. Its high-pitched whistle could have called every dog in the world.

Moldy mozzarella! This is no storm! This is a hurricane!

I thought, nervously tugging the fur on top of my head, What rotten luck to be caught by the storm just now. We had only two or three more days before we would hit Treasure Island!

Each time the boat rocked, I could hear my seasick cousin moaning down in his, cabin. *Serves him right,* I thought. It seems Trap had "accidentally" forgotten to mention he was never a captain of a ship — he was a cook!

Night came, and things got even worse. We couldn't make out the direction of the waves in the dark. The *Lucky Lady* rocked back and forth like my uncle Nibbles dancing at a family wedding. We were soaked through to our tonsils. Dawn came, and **THE SEA was still raging.**

Suddenly, disaster struck. *A gust of wind* tore down the mast. The *Lucky Lady* TILTED ON ITS SIDE, AND WATER BEGAN TO FLOOD IN. We were sinking!

THE TRUNK OF MANY WONDERS

I found myself adrift in the ICY sea. I thrashed about for a long time, spitting out salty water. Monster-sized waves kept rolling me around. I felt like I was stuck in the rinse cycle of a GIANT WASHING MACHINE.

Suddenly, I caught sight of a little gray furry thing.

"Benjamin!!!" I cried, grabbing him by his tail.

As if by magic, the wind stopped. I looked around. The *Lucky Lady* had vanished without a trace. We needed something to hold on to. And then I saw it.

Well, happy birthday to me (and to

Benjamin, too, of course)! It was my **TRUNK**! I grabbed it with all my mousely strength.

Safe! We were safe!

Standing upright on the trunk, I scanned the horizon for Thea and Trap. Not a head or tail in sight. By afternoon, I was beginning to lose hope. But then I spied two very, very small dots in the distance. My heart beat so **FAST** even my fur stood up to see what all the fuss was about.

"Thea! Trap!" I shouted at the top of my lungs. It was my sister and my cousin, all right! I paddled out to them, paws flying.

"Take hold of my tail!" I shouted as I dragged them in.

"I really thought it was the end, Cousin!" panted Trap, collapsing onto the **TRUNK**.

Thea wrapped her tail around mine. "Big brother, I'm so glad you're okay!" She sighed. I hugged her tight. Tears rolled down Thea's wet, furry face.

Trap, was crying, too, for different reasons. "The *Emerald Eye*," he sobbed. "We'll never find it now, without the map!"

I glanced at my sister. For some reason, she was grinning. "Did someone say map?" She slipped a paw under her sweater, and out came the **crumpled-up** map!

"CRUNCHY CHEESE CHUNKS!" shouted Trap. He threw his paws in the air like he'd just won tickets to the Supermouse Bowl.

Hooray!
Hooray!
Hooray!
Hooray!!
Hooray
Hooray!
Hooray!
Hooray!
Hooray
Hooray!
Hooray!

Just then, Benjamin opened his eyes.

"How are you doing, my little mousie?" I asked him.

"Uncle! Is it you, Uncle Geronimo?" he murmured.

"Yes, my dear little Benjamin, it's me," I whispered warmly. "Everything is going to be all right now, you'll see."

Hooray!

Hooray!!

Hooray!

Hooray!

Hooray!

Hooray!

Hooray!

GOOD-BYE, SILK PAJAMAS!

Thea tried to review the situation.

"According to my calculations, we should be right near Treasure Island," she said. Then she pointed to a black-and-white dot in the sky. "A pelican! That means we are really close!"

Just then, Trap gave a loud shriek. I **jumped**. "What is it? Do you always have to shout like that?" I complained.

"I've got an **idea!**" he squeaked in my ear. Then he grabbed the **TRUNK'S** handle, trying to **lift** the lid.

"What are you doing? Do you want to throw us all back in the water?" I protested.

Trap was waving his arms around in the air.

"Why are you flapping your arms?" I shouted at him. "Are you going to tell us you can fly now, too?"

Trap kept waving excitedly. "*Pajamas . . . belt . . . blue stripes!*" he cried.

Finally, he managed to rip my comfy blue-and-white-striped pajamas out of the trunk. Then he tore them into two pieces!

"I REALLY AM A GENIUS! I am so clever it frightens me at times!" My cousin giggled. He was beginning to sound like a rat who's eaten one too many slices of American cheese. "We'll just use this rag to make a sail!"

"Rag? You call this a rag?" I screamed. "These are my silk pajamas with silver buttons! They cost me a fortune! They have my initials embroidered in gold!"

"Well, isn't that just like you to be so selfish." Trap sighed. "We're talking about a treasure here, and you're worried about your pajamas. **Geronimoid**, you amaze me!!"

I gnashed my teeth together. "Don't call me **Geronimoid**! My name is Geronimo! Geronimo, got it?!"

There was nothing left to do now but rig up Trap's pajama sail and take off. We were all terribly thirsty.

"My tongue feels like it got stuck in the sandbox at Scampertown Park," mumbled Trap. "I would give anything for some **ice cream**. Do you remember that ice-cream parlor The Icy Rat? The **AIR-CONDITIONING** in that place was always on full blast. You could freeze your

fur off just waiting for your hot-cheese sundae!"

Sweat dripped down my snout. Why did Trap have to go on about ice cream? I was starting to have visions of cheddar-cheese sugar cones floating on the water.

The next morning, a peal of thunder SHOOK the sky. I licked my snout, and it was covered with drops. Drops of water! The rain was pelting down like the jet of a shower. I swallowed the drops that fell on my tongue. I was in mouse heaven! Thea and Trap *danced* their paws off. Then, as *suddenly* as it had come, the rain stopped. We hugged. Then, winding our tails together, we squeaked:

"Friends together! Mice forever!"

Ben was the first one to reach the island.

LAAAAAND HO!

Finally, at sunrise on the eighth day of our pajama-sailing adventure, I heard someone squeaking,"**Laaaaand ho!**"

I stared at the island emerging from the waves. It got closer and closer. The sea flowed beneath us like an emerald-green carpet.

Ben was the first one to reach the island. The beach was covered with fine white sand. When my cousin landed, he flopped onto his belly and kissed the ground. Then he turned toward us, snout covered in sand. He looked like he'd just eaten a doughnut.

"Ratlings," he said. "No one is going to unglue me from this spot!

From now on I am a land mouse, not a sea mouse! And proud of it!"

EMERALD-GREEN

Deep *green* water, *green* plants, *green* grass, *green* trees. **TREASURE ISLAND** would be the perfect place for a Saint Patrat's Day party! The whole place looked like nature had colored it with a magical *green* paintbrush. We dragged the **TRUNK** onto the beach and began to explore the island.

We worked hard to cut a path through the thick plants and shrubs. We struggled over gigantic **rocks** covered in slippery **moss**. Then we tried following a line of leafy green palm trees. It was tough going.

We had been hiking for about ten minutes when we heard a noise. It sounded like running water. No, not just plain old

running water like when you fill
up the bathtub. This was LOUD
running water.

We turned the corner and there it
was . . . a wonderful, beautiful **waterfall!**
It rushed down from the top of a
cliff into a lake of crystal-clear water.
On the other side of the waterfall
stood a tree so tall even the clouds
had to step aside to make room for it.

Its enormous **ROOTS** clung to the ROCKS like a cat with a tuna sandwich. The island was **THICK** with fruit-bearing trees. Bananas, mangoes, and papayas hung over our heads. For a minute, I felt like I was strolling through the supermarket. I picked some *fruit* and took it back to my friends. Benjamin shrieked with joy as he hurled himself onto a big slice of papaya.

GE-RO

"*Gerry* has brought us lunch!" shouted Thea, jumping out of the water.

"Hooray! Way to go, *Geronimouse*. I'm starved!" squeaked Trap.

"Geronimouse? Geronimouse? How many times do I have to say it? If I've told you once I've told you a hundred times . . . my name is . . .

-NI-MO!"

Why, why, oh, why do I always have to repeat it?

LINE UP!

That night, we slept in the big **TREE** on the other side of the waterfall. We lay in a hollow where two branches joined. Our backs were pressed together for support. Still, I didn't sleep a wink. I was too afraid of falling out of the tree.

Next morning, we all gathered for a meeting. We had to decide who would be in charge on the island.

"We will vote by a show of paws!" I said.

Of course, Trap voted for himself. Thea voted for me. And Benjamin and I gave our votes to Thea.

My sister cleared her throat. "Friends, I want you to know you won't regret your choice," she said, wiping away a small tear. Then . . .

"**Line up** now!" she shouted. "I will begin by assigning your duties. At noon, you will report to me . . . and you will be on time! When I say noon, I mean noon! Not one minute before, not one minute later!

Is THAT QUITE CLEAR?

I don't hear you!!!!"

"Ugh! She's already gotten a swollen head! I knew I was right to vote for myself," muttered Trap under his whiskers.

Thea was walking up and down the beach. "We shall build a shelter under the **TREE**. It will take us two, no, three days to finish it. Then we leave in search of the *Emerald Eye!*"

Trap's eyes lit up again. "The treasure! Now you're talking!" He grinned.

In the meantime, Thea had grabbed a sheet of paper and was scribbling down tasks for all of us. "Geronimo, you will take care of provisions. You'll gather fruit, berries, and roots. You'll also fish for crabs. Trap, you will be head chef."

"**EXCELLENT CHOICE, BOSS**! Just wait till you see what tasty dishes I can prepare! Whisker-licking good!" said my cousin cheerfully.

"Benjamin, you will help me build our shelter under the **TREE**," Thea continued, without missing a beat. "And now, get going!"

Friends together! Mice forever!

FROM MY DIARY

Dear Diary,
I am writing on this banana leaf because there is no paper left. It took us three days to build our hut under the big tree. What a project! We all pitched in, with Thea squeaking out orders like an army general. I think she's getting a little _too_ into her job as leader — but that's just between you and me, Diary. I don't want to end up on bathroom duty . . . or worse!

Speaking of bathrooms, we built one in our hut. We made a giant wooden wheel to run the water up from the stream.

Of course, Thea and Trap are forever fighting over who gets to use the bathroom first. In fact, I can hear them screaming right now. Everything is different on this island, but those two never change! Good-bye, dear Diary, I have to rush to the kitchen. Tonight it's my turn to wash the dishes.

Yours, Geronimo

P.S. I have realized that an adventurous life is definitely not my cup of tea. Oh, how I miss my comfy, safe home!

CHEESE SLICES

That night, Thea stayed up very late. I wondered what my sister had up her sleeve this time. You just never know with that mouse.

Early the next morning, while we were having breakfast, Thea arrived, out of breath. "Hooray! I did it!" she cried, waving the map.

Trap jumped. "Do you have to **scream** so early in the morning?" he shouted. "You know I'm not awake until I've had my cup of steamed cheese (two sugars, hold the milk). Now, what is it?"

Thea jumped onto the table and cleared her throat. "I have discovered . . ." she began. "Drumroll, please."

"**What??**" shouted Trap, grabbing her by the tail.

Thea shot Trap a smug smile. "First I determined our position, using the astrolabe. Then I checked it with a triangulation . . . and worked out the logarithm. . . ."

"ASTROLAMP? STRANGULATION? CONGARHYTHM?" snorted Trap. "Do you mind speaking English? I hate it when you **use such big words!**"

My sister pointed to the map. "First we have to head north toward *More Water Bay.* Then we go around *What's the Point Peak* and head toward *Molehill Mountain.* There we'll find the *Fleariddenfur River.* We follow the river to *Hard as Nails Hill.* And from there, it should be as easy as pie to find the *Emerald Eye!*"

At the mention of the word *emerald*, Trap put his arm around Thea.

"Oh, my little cousin, let me be the first to congratulate you." He beamed. "Did anyone ever tell you that you are a real **genius**? So where did you say the treasure is exactly?"

Thea snorted. "What is the matter with you? Are your eyes covered with ⓒⓗⓔⓔⓢⓔ slices? Look here at the map," she squeaked, flapping it under Trap's snout. "There is an **X** on it as big as the moon over Mouse Island!"

Trap just smiled and stroked Thea's paw. "My dear, sweet, kind, beautiful, charming little cousin," he said. "I suggest we leave tomorrow morning, no, maybe tonight. As a matter of fact, I could be ready to leave **RIGHT NOW!**"

"Wait a minute, wait a minute," I jumped in. "We have to map out our route, calculate the times and the stages of our trip."

Trap was getting more and more frantic.

"What times . . . what stages? This sly mouse here has already organized everything. We are leaving and that's that!" he squeaked. Then he and Thea put their heads together and began discussing the details of the journey.

Of all the nerve! It seemed as if I was already left out! Meanwhile, my nephew sat munching the last Cheesy Chew with a dreamy expression on his face. "Treasure, real honest-to-goodmouse treasure . . ." he murmured.

ONE SKULL

The plan was to leave at six o'clock the next morning. But by four o'clock, my cousin was already up and about.

"Ratoons, we are leaving!" Trap shouted through a **MEGAPHONE** made of banana leaves.

Thea grabbed a coconut and hurled it at his head. "Do you realize what time it is?" she shrieked, chasing him around our **SHELTER**. "When I catch you, I'm going to use your fur to make earmuffs!"

Trap just giggled. "If you don't hurry, I am going to leave without you!" he shouted through the megaphone. "I am ready to rock! **READY** to roll! **READY** to rumble!

READY to party! Ready to GO! GO! GO!"

Thea was tearing at her whiskers in a rage. **"You are the one who brought him along!"** she yelled at me.

If you don't hurry, I am leaving without you!

I wanted to say, "Actually, it was your idea," but I stopped myself. The look in my sister's eyes was MURDEROUS.

We set out in single file. We marched all day long. By evening, we came to **WHAT'S THE POINT PEAK**. Thea pointed at the map. "We have reached the location of the first skull. Listen to this secret message:

"IF YOU FIND A BIG ROCK
THE COLOR OF CHEESE,
DON'T RUN AROUND,
DON'T EVEN SNEEZE!"

Somewhat puzzled, I looked around. "This must be the rock on the map," I said, pointing to a round, cheddar-colored boulder. "It looks good enough to eat!"

I took a few steps forward. "But there is nothing to see here. Just some sand. Actually, a whole bunch of san —"

I didn't get to finish my sentence. I was beginning to sink.

"Look at me!" I giggled. "Hee! Hee! **Hee-hee!** Look, the sand has reached my ankles . . . no, my knees!"

THEA'S EYES OPENED WIDE. SHE WAS NOT LAUGHING.

"Geronimo! I have bad news for you!" she called.

"Hmm? What bad news?" I asked, watching the funny sand.

"Geronimo," my sister squeaked, "I think that's **quicksand**!"

I gulped. "Thundering cattails! Quicksand?" I shrieked. "*Help!*"

The sand had already reached my bellybutton.

"Stop flapping your arms!" shouted Thea, holding her paw out.

But I kept flapping and flapping. "Heeeeelp!" I shouted as the sand reached my ears.

Trap raced over carrying a long green vine from a nearby tree.

"Grab hold of this, Cousin, if you ever want to squeak again!" he cried.

Two Skulls

Once again, Trap had saved my life.

"Why, oh, why did I ever agree to take this trip? I must be losing my marbles! When I get back to New Mouse City, my fur will have turned white from all these scares," I mumbled.

"If we ever get back, that is," added Trap in a grim voice.

He always knew how to cheer me up.

The next morning, we crossed *Molehill Mountain* and marched along the banks of the *Fleariddenfur River*. Finally, we sighted **Hard as Nails Hill**.

"This is it," announced Thea. "The place of the TWO SKULLS."

I shivered. What would we find this time? More quicksand? Exploding boulders? Grouchy Grandma Onewhisker with a plate of her disgusting Swiss cheese muffins? I looked around. We were in a clearing with one very tall tree standing in the center. It was loaded with big yellow fruit that looked sort of like pineapples.

Thea read aloud the secret message about the TWO SKULLS:

"BEWARE OF THE HONEY TREE,
ITS FRUITS ARE KNOWN TO SING,
LISTEN, BUT DO NOT TOUCH,
OR YOU WILL FEEL THE STING!"

Trap stepped forward. "Fruits that sting? How ridiculous! Let me take one of them, ratoons! I'll knock one down with a stone and then we'll see!"

STOP!

"**STOP!** Don't do it!" I shrieked.

"Don't worry, **Gerrykins**." My cousin laughed. "So what if they sting? Anyway, I'll just avoid touching them. See?

Hee-hee-hee!"

He pitched a stone right at the biggest fruit in the center.

"Don't call me **Gerryk —** " I started to say, but I stopped in midsentence.

The *yellow fruit* was not a giant pineapple. It wasn't even a fruit. It was a giant beehive!

"**Help!**" we screamed together. The beehive was oozing **thick** golden honey. Within seconds, swarms of bees flew out from the honeycombs hanging on the branches.

"Hurry! To the river!" shouted my sister.

We raced to the river with the bees right on our tails.

Then we dove headfirst into the water. The current carried us downstream. When we reached the bank, the bees were gone.

Thea pulled out her map. "Let's see, to our left is *Hard as Nails Hill*, and in front of us is *Pirate's Peak*. That means if we go forward we'll hit the **THREE SKULLS!"**

THREE SKULLS

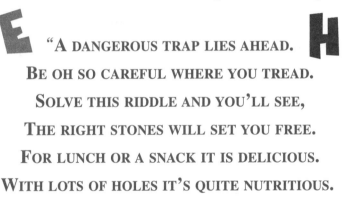

In front of us lay a narrow path made of stones. Each stone had a letter engraved on it. Thea read aloud the message on the map.

"A DANGEROUS TRAP LIES AHEAD.
BE OH SO CAREFUL WHERE YOU TREAD.
SOLVE THIS RIDDLE AND YOU'LL SEE,
THE RIGHT STONES WILL SET YOU FREE.
FOR LUNCH OR A SNACK IT IS DELICIOUS.
WITH LOTS OF HOLES IT'S QUITE NUTRITIOUS.
WHITE OR YELLOW,
SHARP OR MELLOW,
LEAVE SOME FOR OTHERS,
BE A GOOD FELLOW!"

I reread the riddle several times. My cousin tapped his paw impatiently.

"Well, Mr. Newspaper Mouse, **you work with words**. What does it mean?" he asked. His paw kept tapping faster and faster. "Well, come on, what are you waiting for? We don't have all day, you know."

Trying to ignore my cousin, I stared at the riddle. The answer was right on the tip of my tongue. What has lots of holes? What is white or yellow and delicious? Suddenly, I clapped my paws together. "It's cheese!" I shrieked with glee. "You must jump on the letters spelling out the word CHEESE!"

Before we could stop him, Trap hopped onto the stone engraved with the letter C. Then he hopped on the H, then the E, and then the S.

Trap hopped onto the first stone.

"Look out!" the rest of us screamed.

Spelling has never been one of my cousin's strong points. Of course, there are two E's in the middle of **CHEESE**!

The minute Trap set his paw on the wrong stone it *gave way*, and down he went.

I peered into the hole. It was ... *very deep!*

A foul-smelling odor rose from it.

Wait a minute. I could just make out something at the bottom. Uh-oh. I was looking at a bunch of bones!

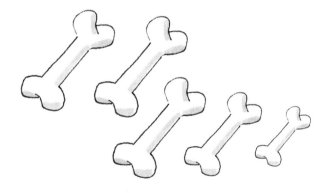

POOR TRAP!

"Poor Uncle Trap!" sobbed Benjamin.

"Poor Cousin. We won't even be able to visit his grave," murmured Thea, wiping away a tear.

"He was such a great mouse. Do you remember when he saved your life at sea, Uncle?" cried Benjamin.

Even I felt terrible. "How could I ever forget?" I moaned. "Trap saved my life not once, but twice. The first time at sea and the second time from the quicksand. He was so courageous!"

He was so courageous!

Then Thea added softly, "Well, let's be honest, sometimes he could be a bit of a *pain*."

Benjamin jumped right in. "Actually, now that I think about it, poor Uncle Trap could be pretty *annoying*."

I stood up and dusted the dirt off my paws. "In fact, I think he was totally *obnoxious* at times!"

"**A PAIN? ANNOYING? OBNOXIOUS?**" a voice called out from the hole.

We peered into the deep pit. Trap was hanging by his pants from a tree root.

"Hang on, Trap! **we are coming** to the rescue!" I called.

We lifted him out in no time. Trap looked a little pale. Still, he sounded just as irritating as ever.

"You know, I heard all the bad things you said about me," he said. Then he smiled.

"But I guess you said some nice things, too. Especially you, **Gerrymug**. In fact, Geronimiss, I could give you a kiss! Hey, that's pretty good," he giggled. Hee!Hee!

I groaned. Why, oh, why had we pulled him out of that hole!

"Geronimiss, I could give you a kiss!"

GOLD DOUBLOONS?

We started hiking toward the **X** again. According to Thea's map, we had almost reached the *Emerald Eye*. Trap practically skipped the rest of the way. I'd never seen him so excited. Well, there was that time he won a free cheeseburger at Burger Mouse. . . .

Trap's voice interrupted my thoughts. "Hey, Cousinkins, do you think we'll find other things besides the *Emerald Eye*? I mean, you're the expert on this stuff, right? Could we find jewels or lots of **money**?"

"Well, we could find some old coins," I answered. "Maybe we might find **gold doubloons.**

They have a picture of the cat prince Meow Iron Claw, also known as Snarls the Mouse Muncher, on them."

Trap did a little dance. "Doubloons! Doubloons! Gold doubloons! I just love the sound of that word!" He chuckled.

Meanwhile, Thea was checking the map. She pointed straight ahead.

"That's it!" she announced. "The Emerald Eye should be right in front of us!"

Trap ran ahead. Then he stopped. He looked around, confused.

"I don't see any emerald here. All I see is water!" he squeaked.

For once, my cousin was telling the truth. On the exact spot where we were supposed to find the Emerald Eye, there was a deep lake!

"ASTROLAMP? STRANGULATION? CONGARHYTHM?" snorted Trap furiously.

"But this is exactly where the **X** is on my map," Thea murmured.

"If it is the right place, then we are on the wrong island! And it's all your fault!" Trap cried, chasing after Thea.

I sighed, my head between my paws. Benjamin sat beside me, looking sad. Just then, I heard leaves rustling.

The sound was coming from the forest nearby.

"Sssssh! Keep quiet, everyone!" I whispered. "Something back here is moving!"

We all strained our ears to listen.

"Something . . . or someone!" whispered Trap in a shaky voice. He looked at us. "Let's see. Who can go check things out? Ben is too young. Thea can't be of any help because she is a **FEMALE**. And it's really only right that I stay behind to look after those two. So that only leaves you, Geronimo. Better get going!" he concluded, pushing me toward the bushes where the noises were coming from.

At that moment, Thea sprang into action. "Just because I'm female doesn't mean I can't take care of things!" she shrieked. She grabbed her knife with two paws and charged toward the bushes.

"SHOW YOURSELF, IF YOU DARE!" she squeaked, moving aside a few leaves.

Little Benjamin trembled beside me. Trap whimpered. Even my tough-talking sister was shaking.

I chewed on my whiskers. I imagined a pack of ferocious wild tomcats or maybe lions on the other side of the bushes. So this is how it would end? We would all become snacks for some mouse-munching monsters? All of our sailing and swimming and hiking and sweating for nothing? It was almost too much to bear. I closed my eyes.

When I opened them again, I saw the strangest sight. In front of us stood a group of animals. No, not a band of drooling tomcats. Not a pack of roaring lions. It was a party of **mice**. They were dressed in bathing suits. Some had cameras and camcorders.

One of the mice stepped forward. "Hello. Are you guests of the resort?" he asked.

"RESORT? WHAT RESORT?"
we all squeaked at the same time.

"**RaTliN's** Tropical Resort and Health Spa, of course," the mouse said, giving us a strange look.

SNIP!
SNAP!

For a moment, I thought maybe I was just having a bad dream. **I PINCHED MYSELF.** The mice in the bathing suits were still standing there.

At last, Trap spoke. "**RATLIN'S** Tropical Resort," he repeated. "Do you mean this **IS NOT** a **DESERTED** island?"

The guide looked at us with curiosity.

"Deserted island? You should see the mounds of rodents on the beach," he said. "This is our busiest time of year!"

Trap turned to Thea, fuming. "It's bad enough that you brought me to the wrong island. But did you have to bring me to a tourist trap?!"

I couldn't believe it. I felt a lump of despair in my throat — like a mouse being served at the Grand Cat Buffet.

Meanwhile, the tourists were staring at us in amazement. With our **ratty** fur and **torn** clothing, they didn't know what to make of us!

A shy-looking mouse with big ears approached Thea. "Um, Miss, did you just take one of Ratlin's SURVIVAL classes?" he asked.

Thea stared at him. For a minute, she looked like a mouse caught by a flashlight. Then my sister snapped to attention. "Survival lessons?" she repeated. "Why, do I look like a rodent who needs lessons? Take a look at this knife. I can chop a rat's tail in two faster than you can twitch your whiskers. Snip! Snap!"

She cut a tree branch in two with one clean blow. Her audience shuddered, hypnotized.

"Can I walk you back to the **resort**?" the mouse with the big ears asked my sister. "I would love to take you to dinner tonight. I know a great little restaurant right on the beach!"

"We'll see, my dear, we'll see," squeaked Thea, flattered.

I shook my head. Benjamin and I set out toward the resort. Trap just stared off

into space. "But the treasure . . ." he repeated over and over. "The treasure . . ."

FASTEN YOUR SEAT BELTS!

After listening to our amazing adventures, the manager of **RATLIN'S** Resort got us four first-class seats on the first flight back to New Mouse City. Well, actually three seats, since Thea had decided to stay a few more days.

"He is such a deeeear!" Thea had shrieked about her new, big-eared friend. "I have never met such a charming mouse! He adores me, and he is sooo romantic! *Geronimo*, why don't you stay for a little longer, too?"

"**I want to go home!** I just want to go home!" I kept telling her.

The time to leave finally came. "Now boarding!" blasted the loudspeaker at the airport. We climbed onto the plane.

"All rodents, please fasten your seat belts!" the pilot requested.

A *pretty* flight attendant with **dark brown** fur walked down the aisle, passing out slices of tasty Swiss cheese.

"HAVE FUN on your vacation?" asked the mouse seated next to me.

Fun *wouldn't exactly be my first word to describe it,* I thought. *How about* disaster? *Or* nightmare? But I nodded anyway. "Fun," I grumbled. **"LOADS OF FUN."**

Trap was back to his **usual self**. I heard him flirting with the flight attendant.

He told her he was *an expert sailor.*

Then he began telling her about our **ADVENTURE**.

I missed most of the details. I was too busy looking at the view outside my window. This was the first time I had seen the island from above. It was quite a sight. Right in the middle of the ISLAND was a *lake as green as an emerald*! And, of course, the lake was exactly where the treasure was supposed to be on Thea's map.

Now, that was odd. From up in the sky, the lake looked just like an **emerald-green** eye. Eye? Emerald?

"Holey cheese!" I squeaked excitedly. Benjamin, who had fallen sound asleep, woke

up with a squeak.

"**LOOK**!" I shouted, pulling Trap's tail. I jumped out of my seat and pointed out the window. "It's the *Emerald Eye!*" I shrieked.

A frail white-haired rat waved her book at me. "Shhh!" she said, glaring. Other passengers threw me dirty looks. Oh, well, guess I wouldn't be winning the most popular passenger award.

"So that is the treasure shown on the *map*!" I cried, ignoring my newfound enemies.

My cousin just snorted. "Gerryboy, to me a treasure is something you can spend! All you can do with that treasure is wash your socks in it!"

I sighed, sinking back into my seat. The shimmering *green* lake in the middle of

the island **moved farther and farther away**.
Benjamin laid his tiny head on my shoulder.
"I think the *Emerald Eye* is a wonderful
treasure, Uncle," he said. "It's the most
beautiful treasure I've ever seen!"

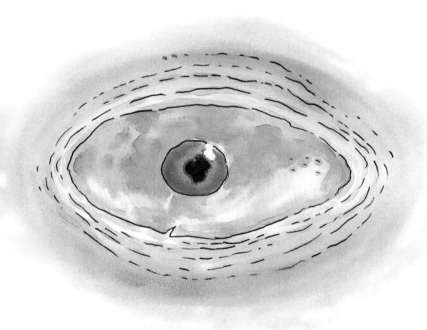

MEGA HUGE FRIDGE!

IT WAS SO NICE TO BE HOME AGAIN!

Clean sheets, a **HOT** shower, and my **MEGA** huge fridge stuffed with the best cheeses a mouse can buy!

Today I bumped into Trap. "You have such a way with words. Why don't you slap together an adventure story about the treasure hunt?" he suggested.

"Are you kidding? I am a busy mouse! I run a newspaper! It's unthinkable! It's impossible! It's ridiculous!" I replied.

That evening, though, I leafed through my travel diary. So much to write about, what an adventure! Maybe for once Trap had come up with a good **idea**. . . .

My mega huge fridge was stuffed with the best cheeses!

TENNIS
TOP CLUB

Six months have gone by since the day we returned from our trip. I followed Trap's advice and wrote the book. I published it, too. And you'll never guess what happened. It **SOLD**! Like catnip at the Meowville Movie Theater!

The book is already on the *bestseller list* here in New Mouse City.

"Now, this is what I call a real treasure!"

shouted my cousin, waving his check in the air. I figured it was only right to give him some money from the book. After all, he was a big part of the adventure. (Even if his was mostly the annoying part!)

To celebrate my success, I invited Silky Fur, a *very* pretty lady friend of mine, to the Tennis Top Club. "I couldn't put the book down, you know. I never knew you were so brave!" whispered Silky Fur in my ear.

I was beginning to think our adventure might have been worth it after all.

HELLO, GERRY?

rriing, rrriing

At the crack of dawn one morning, I got a call from Thea. "**Gerry**, get ready for an **UN-BE-LIEV-ABLE** piece of news! Guess what I discovered today?" she squeaked.

"How on earth would I know?" I grumbled, crawling back into bed with the phone.

"Another map. You know what I am talking about!" my sister insisted.

"No, I don't. What are you talking about? What map?"

"The same as last time! Do you remember The Mouse House? Cheddar ravioli? Extra-spicy sauce? Don't let me say any more," she demanded, sounding mysterious.

The Mouse House?

Cheddar ravioli?

Extra-spicy sauce?

Another map?

I threw back the covers and jumped out of bed. This could mean only one thing. My crazy sister was planning another trip. "Oh, no! Not this time!" I shrieked into the phone. "Not on your life! Don't you have a boyfriend now? Why don't you ask him to go with you?"

"Who? Old Big Ears?

I got rid of him like moldy cheese." She giggled. "But let's talk about more serious matters.

You wouldn't let me go on my own, would you? You are my older brother, after all. Where is your sense of duty? It could be a very **DAN-GER-OUS** journey! Hello, *Gerry*? *Gerry*, are you still there? *Gerry*, **Gerrrry, Gerrrrry!**" squeaked Thea.

Don't call me Gerry, I wanted to say. *My name is Geronimo, Geronimo Stilton!*

But I had no strength left.

I put the receiver down on my nightstand.

I already knew where this was going to lead. . . .

About the Author

Born in New Mouse City, Mouse Island, Geronimo Stilton is Rattus Emeritus of Mousomorphic Literature and of Neo-Ratonic Comparative Philosophy. For the past twenty years, he has been running *The Rodent's Gazette*, New Mouse City's most widely read daily newspaper.

Stilton was awarded the Ratitzer Prize for his scoop on *The Curse of the Cheese Pyramid*. He has also received the Andersen 2000 Prize for Personality of the Year. One of his bestsellers won the 2002 eBook Award for world's best ratlings' electronic book. His works have been published in 180 countries.

In his spare time, Mr. Stilton collects antique cheese rinds and plays golf. But what he most enjoys is telling stories to his nephew Benjamin.

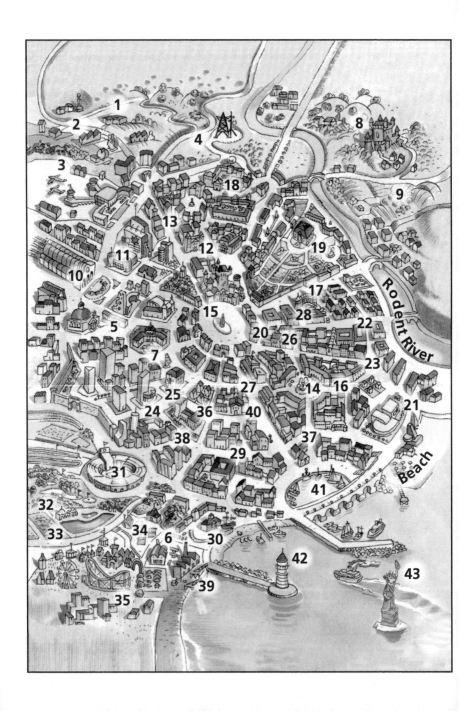

Map of New Mouse City

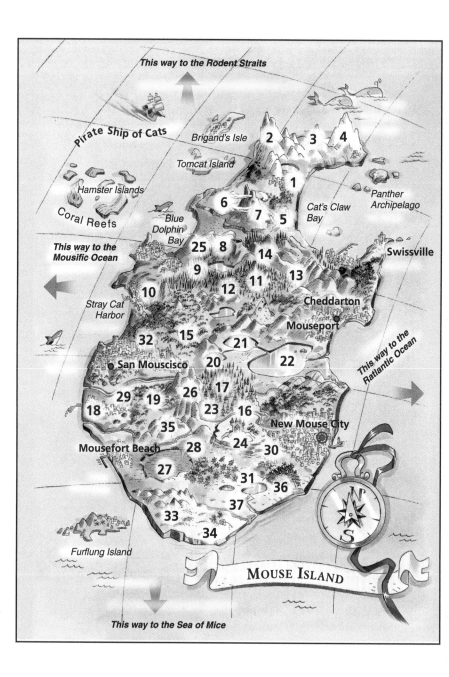

Map of Mouse Island

1.	Big Ice Lake	21.	Lake Lake Lake
2.	Frozen Fur Peak	22.	Lake Lakelakelake
3.	Slipperyslopes Glacier	23.	Cheddar Crag
4.	Coldcreeps Peak	24.	Cannycat Castle
5.	Ratzikistan	25.	Valley of the Giant
6.	Transratania		Sequoia
7.	Mount Vamp	26.	Cheddar Springs
8.	Roastedrat Volcano	27.	Sulfurous Swamp
9.	Brimstone Lake	28.	Old Reliable Geyser
10.	Poopedcat Pass	29.	Vole Vail
11.	Stinko Peak	30.	Ravingrat Ravine
12.	Dark Forest	31.	Gnat Marshes
13.	Vain Vampires Valley	32.	Munster Highlands
14.	Goose Bumps Gorge	33.	Mousehara Desert
15.	The Shadow Line Pass	34.	Oasis of the
16.	Penny Pincher Lodge		Sweaty Camel
17.	Nature Reserve Park	35.	Cabbagehead Hill
18.	Las Ratayas Marinas	36.	Tropical Jungle
19.	Fossil Forest	37.	Rio Mosquito
20.	Lake Lake		

Dear mouse friends,
thanks for reading, and farewell
till the next book.
It'll be another whisker-licking-good
adventure, and that's a promise!

Geronimo Stilton